Alyvia,
You are gorgeous &
Magical Wishes,
Dorothea

Emily's Magical Journey
with Toothena The Tooth Fairy™

This book belongs to:

_____

Written by CoraMarie Clark ★ Illustrated by Val Lawton

STRATEGIX LTD.

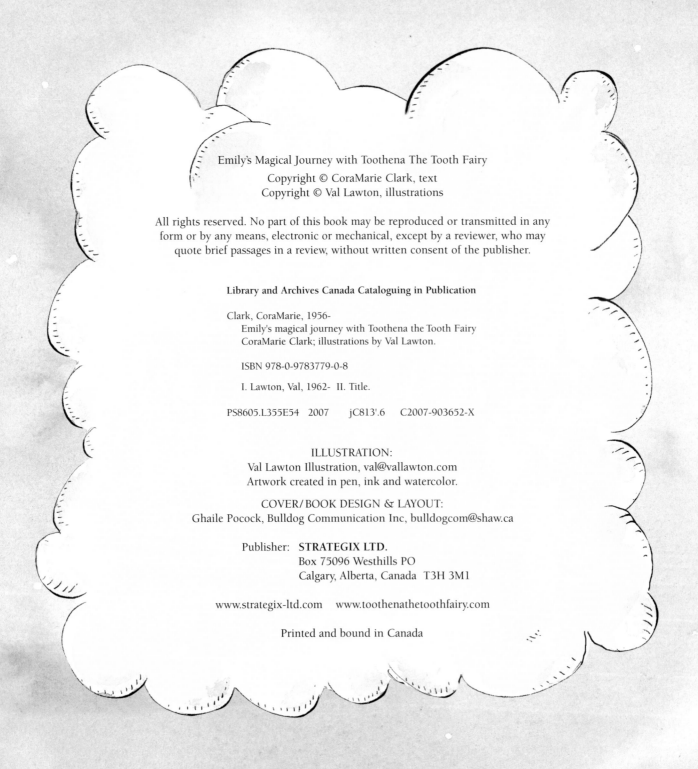

Emily's Magical Journey with Toothena The Tooth Fairy
Copyright © CoraMarie Clark, text
Copyright © Val Lawton, illustrations

Library and Archives Canada Cataloguing in Publication

Clark, CoraMarie, 1956-
    Emily's magical journey with Toothena the Tooth Fairy
    CoraMarie Clark; illustrations by Val Lawton.

ISBN 978-0-9783779-0-8

I. Lawton, Val, 1962- II. Title.

PS8605.L355E54 2007   jC813'.6   C2007-903652-X

ILLUSTRATION:
Val Lawton Illustration, val@vallawton.com
Artwork created in pen, ink and watercolor.

COVER/BOOK DESIGN & LAYOUT:
Ghaile Pocock, Bulldog Communication Inc, bulldogcom@shaw.ca

Publisher: **STRATEGIX LTD.**
              Box 75096 Westhills PO
              Calgary, Alberta, Canada T3H 3M1

www.strategix-ltd.com   www.toothenathetoothfairy.com

Printed and bound in Canada

CoraMarie Clark, Author

*To my precious mother, Mildred Clark,
who dedicated her life to teaching
and enriching people's lives.*

Val Lawton, Illustrator

*To Nicholas and Holly,
my wide-eyed and eternally
enthusiastic children.*

"Are you sure the tooth fairy will find my tooth under my pillow?" Emily asked as her mother tucked her into bed. That morning, after nine days of wiggling, jiggling, and squiggling her tooth, it had finally popped out.

"Yes, my love," Emily's mother replied, checking to make sure Emily's tooth was safe and snug in its place. She gave Emily one more kiss goodnight, wished her sweet dreams, and left the room.

Since she first noticed her loose tooth,
Emily had not been able to stop thinking
about this special time. She was determined
to stay awake all night so she could see
the tooth fairy. Emily wanted to
touch the tooth fairy's wings and
find out what was going to
happen to her tooth.

Emily wondered if the tooth fairy
might be wearing a pale pink dress
with picture perfect polka dots,
or a billowing blue dress
with brilliantly
beaming butterflies.

Once again,
Emily thought about her big question:
What *was* the tooth fairy going
to do with her tooth?

Emily wondered if
there was a mountain
of teeth somewhere
big enough to
slide down.

Or were they given to babies
who had no teeth of their own yet.

Or maybe the tooth fairy
strung the teeth together to make
a pearl necklace like the one
her mother wore. Emily could
hardly wait to find out.

Emily wanted to stay awake,

but she was starting to get sleepy.

As the minutes ticked by, Emily found herself

counting sheep as they joyfully jumped over the fence.

One sheep. Two sheep. Three sheep.

Emily began to giggle...

The sheep were all missing one of their front teeth!

Hearing Emily giggle, her mother called out
that it was time to be quiet and go to sleep.

Emily decided
to close her eyes, squeezing
them tight. After a little while, she felt
a gentle breeze. When she opened her eyes...
the tooth fairy was hovering at the end of her bed.

"Hello, Emily, I'm Toothena."
The tooth fairy had the most
beautiful smile Emily
had ever seen.

She was dressed in
a dreamy pink gown that
seemed to dance when
she moved. A tiara sparkled
in her hair and her magic
wand shimmered
in the dark.

"What are you going to do with my tooth?" blurted Emily.
"Would you like to come to the tooth fairy castle
and see for yourself?" Toothena asked.

Emily nodded and reached up to take the
tooth fairy's hand. She felt herself begin to fly... out
of her bedroom window... and up, up into the starlit sky!
Emily had always wanted to fly. It tickled her
tummy and was even more exciting
than riding a roller coaster!

Moments later, Emily saw the tooth fairy castle.

It was magical!

The moon made the ivory towers glow like sparkling enamel.
Tooth-shaped flags flickered and flowed in the soft breeze.

Walking through the garden outside the castle,
Emily saw flowers everywhere. Suddenly, a big firefly
flew out of a red heart-shaped flower
and swooped towards them.

As it got closer, Emily realized it wasn't a firefly
at all... it was a glittering fairy!

"Meet Twinkles, my helper.
She is the keeper of the castle,"
  Toothena said.

  Twinkles was so tiny she could fit
in the palm of Emily's hand. She had
  dazzling wings and long curly hair.
Breathless, Emily watched the tooth fairy hold
  out her tooth. Twinkles floated in the air, sprinkling fairy
  dust on it, while Toothena whispered:

> As you take this noble flight,
> Make a wish come true tonight.
> Tickety-Toothety, Brushety-Bite,
> Sparkle everything in sight!

Then Toothena tossed Emily's
tooth up into the midnight sky,
where it flashed brilliantly,
like fireworks, and
became a STAR!

A big, bright, twinkling star
called Emily. She could hardly
believe it! Now she could wish
on her very own star!

"Emily, would you like to see
inside the castle?" Toothena asked.
Wide-eyed, Emily whispered
wondrously, "Yes, please."

Emily tiptoed into one of the
bedrooms and squealed with delight!
She jumped onto the bed
made of fluffy white clouds.
It was so soft, it smelled
so good, and... it... felt...
so... dreamy...

When Emily awoke, she was in
her own bed. She reached under her
pillow for her tooth. It was gone!
In its place were two shiny coins.

Emily ran to the window.
Look! There was the Emily
Star, shining brightly!

Now, every night when Emily
looked at all the twinkling stars from
all the boys and girls around the world,
she would always remember her magical
journey with Toothena the tooth fairy.

TOOTH CHART

_____

Child's Name

	Tooth Comes In	Tooth Lost	Treasure From The Tooth Fairy
	age	age	treasure
	age	age	treasure
	age	age	treasure
	age	age	treasure
	age	age	treasure
	age	age	treasure
	age	age	treasure
	age	age	treasure
	age	age	treasure
	age	age	treasure

AVERAGE AGE	Teeth Come In		Teeth Lost	
	UPPER	LOWER	UPPER	LOWER
Central Incisor	6-12 mos.	5-10 mos.	6-7 yrs.	6-7 yrs.
Lateral Incisor	8-13 mos.	10-16 mos.	7-9 yrs.	7-8 yrs.
Cuspid	16-22 mos.	17-23 mos.	10-12 yrs.	9-12 yrs.
First Molar	12-19 mos.	14-18 mos.	9-11 yrs.	9-12 yrs.
Second Molar	24-33 mos.	23-31 mos.	10-12 yrs.	10-13 yrs.

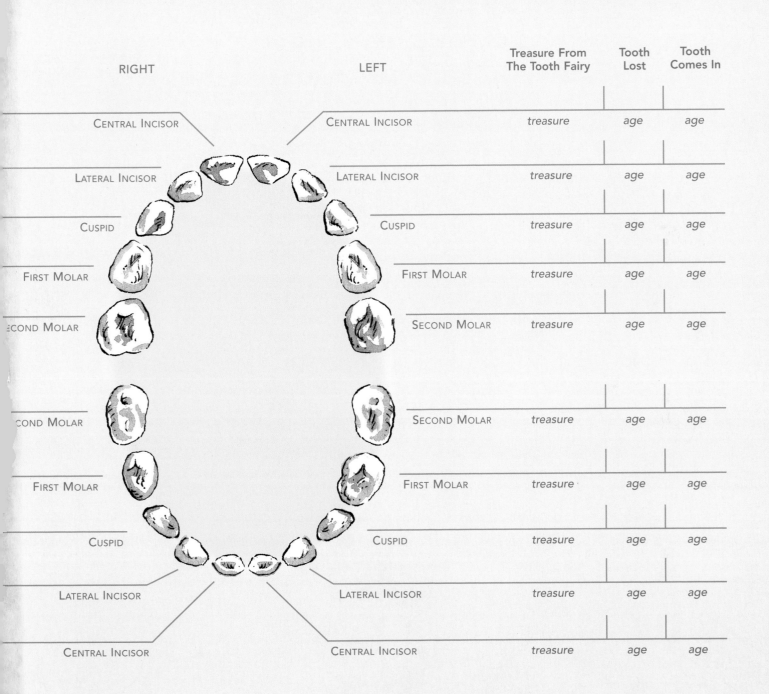

	RIGHT		LEFT	Treasure From The Tooth Fairy	Tooth Lost	Tooth Comes In
					age	age
			Central Incisor	treasure	age	age
	Central Incisor		Lateral Incisor	treasure	age	age
	Lateral Incisor		Cuspid	treasure	age	age
	Cuspid		First Molar	treasure	age	age
	First Molar		Second Molar	treasure	age	age
	Second Molar					
	Second Molar		Second Molar	treasure	age	age
	First Molar		First Molar	treasure	age	age
	Cuspid		Cuspid	treasure	age	age
	Lateral Incisor		Lateral Incisor	treasure	age	age
	Central Incisor		Central Incisor	treasure	age	age

Use this chart to record when your baby teeth come in, when you
lose them and what treasures Toothena the Tooth Fairy brings you.

CoraMarie Clark BSDH MBA

CoraMarie is a speaker, author and consultant in the dental industry,
who along with her three cavity-free children, is fascinated with the tooth fairy.
Her passion to help 100% of children worldwide receive dental care
has inspired her to establish a foundation for children.

Val Lawton

Val has illustrated a number of children's books, including
Starrytime's personalized book, *A Blanket Full of Love,* and Scholastic
Canada's *Mr. Bert's Story Time.* She lives in Calgary, Alberta,
with her husband, two children and a beagle.